TAKE CARE WITH YOURSELF

A young person's guide to understanding, preventing, and healing from the hurts of child abuse.

by Laurie A. White & Steven L. Spencer

Illustrations by Alice Eve Cohen

First Edition - 1982
Second Edition - 1983
Third Edition - 1984

Published by DayStar Press

D id you know that you are a wonderful person? Yes, we mean YOU!

Y ou always deserve to be treated with care. Just because you are you! Some ways people can care for you are: listening to you, spending time with you, making sure you have enough to eat and clothes to wear, and holding you when you need it.

W hen we are treated with care, we feel like the wonderful people we are.

When something hurts us, we have other feelings. We feel sad, angry, afraid or bored.

Everyone feels each of these at times. That's part of being human.

If something hurts you, it's important to let out your feelings. Crying, shaking, laughing or yelling are all ways of letting your feelings go.

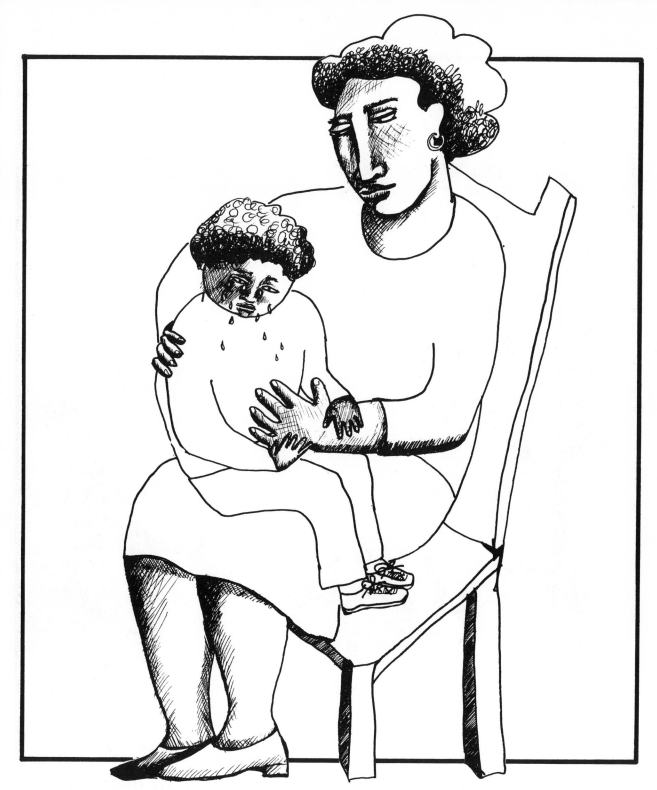

I t's easier to let your feelings go when you feel safe.
Everyone needs to find a safe place. Where is
one of yours?

Sometimes it's hard to find a safe place to go or a safe person to be with when you need to show your feelings. People may try to tell you that showing your feelings isn't okay. They may say things like "only babies cry;" "it isn't nice to be angry;" "there's nothing to be afraid of."

Everyone needs to show their feelings. That's how we heal from our hurts. But what happens when we don't get a chance to heal?

If we don't get a chance to heal, we may feel bad about ourselves.

This can cause us to hurt ourselves or other people.

Many times people can grow up and still feel bad about themselves.

When this happens they may hurt other people, even those they care about. This can happen in many ways.

Some things hurt your body. We call these *physical hurts*. A few of these are:

...Someone hitting you...

...Someone not giving you clothes to wear...
...Someone not feeding you...
...Someone not caring for you when you are sick...

Some things hurt your feelings. We call these *emotional hurts.* A few of these are:

Someone screaming at you and calling you names...

. . .Not having anyone pay attention to you.

Another kind of hurt we call *sexual hurts*. This includes a grown-up touching the sexual or private areas of your body and a grown-up having you touch his or her private areas. *No one* has the right to touch you in *any way* that makes you feel uncomfortable!

For Girls

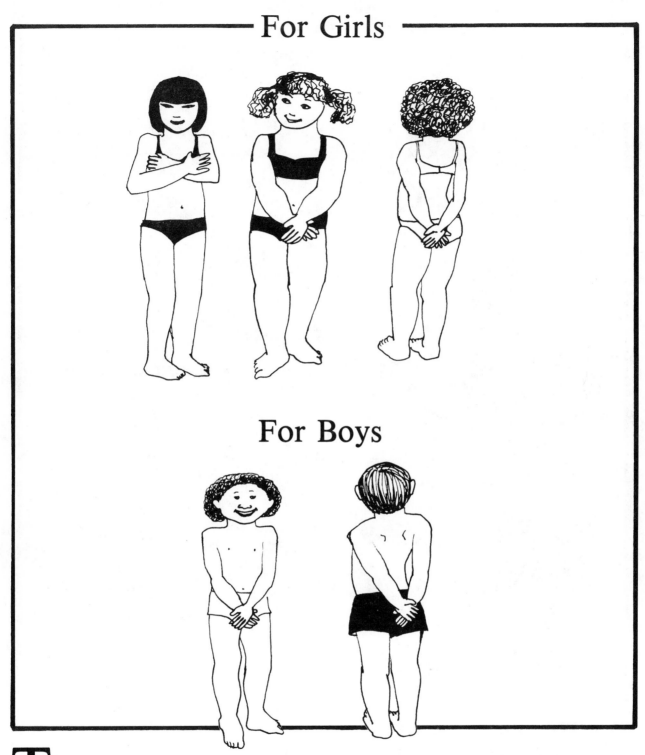

For Boys

These are your sexual or private areas.

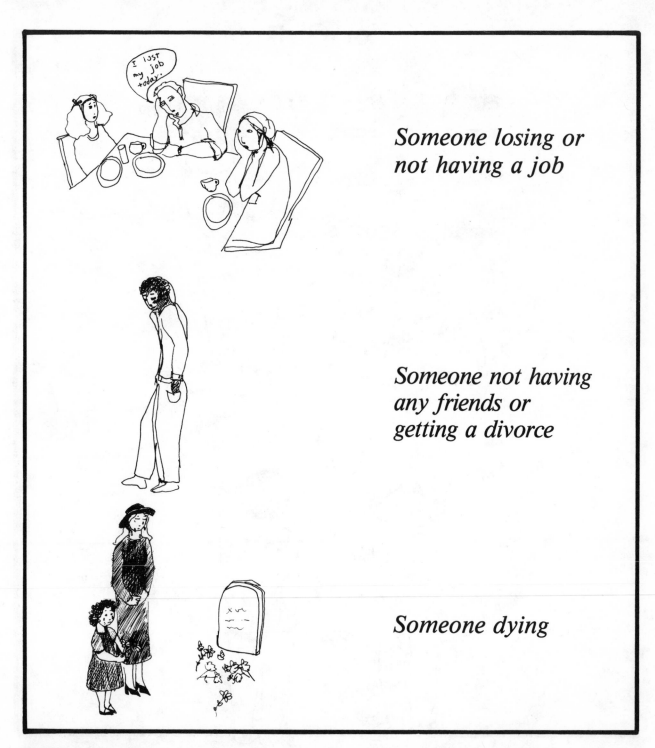

Someone losing or not having a job

Someone not having any friends or getting a divorce

Someone dying

When grown-ups are hurting, they are more likely to hurt others physically, emotionally or sexually.

Someone getting sick

Someone not having any money

Someone drinking or using drugs

The chances are even greater if one of the things above is happening in their lives.

Remember: It is not your fault when grown-ups get upset and hurt someone.

No matter what, *no one* deserves to be hurt —especially you!!

But what if you have been hurt?

What can you do about it?

Tell a safe grown-up about it. Often they can help stop the person who is hurting you.

If they can't help you, tell someone else. Keep trying until you find someone who can help. Things that hurt or make you uncomfortable should *NEVER* be kept secret.

Y ou can try to tell the person who is hurting you to stop (this may not work, but it's worth a try).

If possible, stay away from someone when you think that that person may end up hurting you.

I t may be necessary to call people whose special job it is to protect children. They are called *Children's Protective Services.*

Children's
Protective Services

_____

Police

_____

The law does not allow children to be severely hurt. If you call the police, they may be able to help you. You can call telephone information 1-555-1212 and ask the operator for both of the numbers above.

There are other people who are specially trained to help children and grown-ups heal from their hurtful experiences. If you get a chance to visit with a therapist, it may help you feel better.

Remember: A wonderful person like you deserves the very best. So, TAKE CARE WITH YOURSELF!

For further information or additional copies, contact:

Steven L. Spencer   or   Laurie A. White
4340 Tamarac Trail   1915 Geddes Avenue, #2
Harbor Springs, MI 49740   Ann Arbor, MI 48104
(616) 526-7768   (313) 665-7371

YES! Please send me _____ copies of
TAKE CARE WITH YOURSELF.
at $5.95 postpaid.
I have enclosed a check for _____.
(Make checks payable to Laurie White)

Name _____

Address _____

City _____ State _____ Zip _____

Phone _____ Organization _____

Mail to:
Take Care With Yourself
1915 Geddes Avenue, #2
Ann Arbor, MI 48104

Discounts available for bulk orders. Write for more information.

YES! Please send me _____ copies of
TAKE CARE WITH YOURSELF.
at $5.95 postpaid.
I have enclosed a check for _____.
(Make checks payable to Laurie White)

Name _____

Address _____

City _____ State _____ Zip _____

Phone _____ Organization _____

Mail to:
Take Care With Yourself
1915 Geddes Avenue, #2
Ann Arbor, MI 48104

Discounts available for bulk orders. Write for more information.